Samuel French Acting Edition

Colossal

by Andrew Hinderaker

SAMUELFRENCH.COM   SAMUELFRENCH.CO.UK

FOR PRODUCTION ENQUIRIES

UNITED STATES AND CANADA
Info@SamuelFrench.com
1-866-598-8449

UNITED KINGDOM AND EUROPE
Plays@SamuelFrench.co.uk
020-7255-4302

Each title is subject to availability from Samuel French, depending upon country of performance. Please be aware that *COLOSSAL* may not be licensed by Samuel French in your territory. Professional and amateur producers should contact the nearest Samuel French office or licensing partner to verify availability.

MUSIC USE NOTE

Licensees are solely responsible for obtaining formal written permission from copyright owners to use copyrighted music in the performance of this play and are strongly cautioned to do so. If no such permission is obtained by the licensee, then the licensee must use only original music that the licensee owns and controls. Licensees are solely responsible and liable for all music clearances and shall indemnify the copyright owners of the play(s) and their licensing agent, Samuel French, against any costs, expenses, losses and liabilities arising from the use of music by licensees. Please contact the appropriate music licensing authority in your territory for the rights to any incidental music.

IMPORTANT BILLING AND CREDIT REQUIREMENTS

If you have obtained performance rights to this title, please refer to your licensing agreement for important billing and credit requirements.

COLOSSAL received a rolling world premiere from the National New Play Network (NNPN), with productions at Olney Theatre Center (Olney, Maryland; Jason Loewith, Artistic Director), Mixed Blood Theatre (Minneapolis, Minnesota; Jack Reuler, Artistic Director), Dallas Theater Company (Dallas, Texas; Kevin Moriarty, Artistic Director), Company One (Boston, Massachusetts; Shawn LaCount, Artistic Director), and Southern Rep (New Orleans, Louisiana; Aimee Hayes, Artistic Director).

The inaugural production at Olney Theatre Center was directed by Will Davis, with scenic design by Misha Kachman, costume design by Ivania Stack, lighting design by Colin K. Bills, sound design by Chris Baine, choreography by Christopher D'Amboise, and fight and movement choreography by Ben Cunis. The Production Stage Manager was Josiane M. Lemieux. The cast was as follows:

MIKE	Michael Patrick Thornton
YOUNG MIKE	Joseph Carlson
MARCUS	Jon Hudson Odom
DAMON	Steve Ochoa
JERRY	James Whalen
COACH	KenYatta Rogers
PLAYERS	Sam Faria, Will Hayes, Jeff Kirkman III, Michael Litchfield, Matthew Ward

CHARACTERS

MIKE – Twenty-two. Approximately ten months removed from a catastrophic football injury. Uses a wheelchair. *This role must be played by an artist with a disability.

YOUNG MIKE – Sixteen to twenty-one, at various moments in the play. A dancer, a football player, and an extraordinary physical specimen.

MARCUS – Twenty-one. Young Mike's closest teammate and co-captain of the University of Texas football team.

DAMON – Forties or fifties. Mike's father. Runs a modern dance company and is still an extraordinary mover, though past his prime.

JERRY – Thirties or forties. Responsible for Mike's rehab. A specialist in physical therapy, occupational therapy, and psychology.

COACH – Forties or fifties. Head coach of the University of Texas football team. Cares deeply about his players and believes deeply in the game of football.

PLAYERS – Early twenties. This is our ensemble. At times, they represent Young Mike's teammates at UT; at times his opponents; at times his teammates in high school. There should be at least six players, though ideally the number would be nine.

DAMON SHAW DANCE COMPANY – A modern dance company.

DRUMLINE – Three-to-five Players. *If casting a dance company is not a viable option, the Players can double as dancers, or Young Mike and Damon can perform the halftime show as a duet. Similarly, a single percussionist/recorded drumline can work. But if you have the means for a live drumline...trust me, it's worth it.

AUTHOR'S NOTES

THE VOCABULARIES OF THE PLAY
With the exception of Jerry, no one in this play is terribly comfortable or facile with the spoken word. They're football players and dancers, men who speak principally through movement, silence, and violence.

I've tried to honor that in the storytelling of the piece and hope you'll indulge a few thoughts on:

Dance/Movement
All of the football sequences are told through choreographed movement. The choreography should be inspired by football itself, i.e. it should contain both beauty and brutality.

It's worth looking at some Barry Sanders/Reggie Bush (circa USC) highlights to capture the nimble/beautiful elements of football. As for the brutal violence, check out the hits endured by Kyle Jefferson

(Wisconsin vs. Michigan State) and Reggie Bush (NO vs. Philadelphia – Monday Night).

Silence and Breath

I'd love to explore the idea that we never hear an audible exhale until the very end of the play. For all its wild movement and violence, football is an extraordinarily contained world, where vulnerability is suppressed and secrets are kept. And I don't think there's a true "release" until the play's final moment.

In terms of silence, the script is scored with Quick Beats, Beats, and Long Beats. The play has a driving rhythm (exemplified by a drumline, and a ticking game clock which always counts down). It's most helpful to think of the pauses in terms of music, with:

A (Quick Beat) roughly equivalent to two beats of silence.

A (Beat) equivalent to a full measure of silence.

And a (Long Beat) akin to two full measures of silence.

On the opposite end, a double-dash (--) indicates a lack of any air whatsoever. If it's at the end of a character's line, it signifies overlapping dialogue. The second line should begin on the last, or second-to-last, syllable of the previous line. If a double-dash is in the middle of a character's line, it signifies that the character is accelerating from one thought to another, without pause.

ACKNOWLEDGMENTS

Colossal was developed through workshops at the Kennedy Center, the Alliance Theatre, and the University of Texas. I am deeply indebted to directors Will Davis and Aimee Hayes, choreographers Andrea Beckham and Kelly Maxner, dramaturg Mark Bly, and our entire cast of dancers and football players – most especially Will Brittain and Michael Patrick Thornton.

Additional thanks to Jeff Simon, Jeff Ogden, and Scott Harris, for their football expertise; and to George Hornby and his staff at the Rehab Institute of Chicago.

ONE FINAL NOTE

You're going to want to invest in helmets, mouthguards, and pads – for both performances and rehearsals.

And you may want to include a training program as part of the rehearsal process.

One of the guiding principles of this piece is that everyone in the cast is emotionally and physically exhausted by the end of the performance.

PRE-GAME

(Somewhere in the theater there's a scoreboard.)

(And when the doors open to let the audience in, the clock on the scoreboard starts ticking down from 15:00.)

(As the audience members find their seats, they're met with a blast of drums and the blur of bodies in motion.)

(The football team **PLAYERS** *warm up at full speed: passing routes, up-downs, side-shuffles...)*

(Guided by their **COACH** *and their captains,* **YOUNG MIKE** *and* **MARCUS**.*)*

(And in the middle of the mayhem, dangerously close to the action:)

(There's **DAMON**, *a modern dancer, going through his pre-performance ritual:)*

(A few phrases to test his own impossibly precise footwork.)

(And maybe there's a moment when **YOUNG MIKE** *passes* **DAMON**, *and we notice that their footsteps are perfectly in sync.)*

(Maybe there's a moment between **YOUNG MIKE** *and* **MARCUS**.*)*

(Maybe a moment when **COACH** *pulls* **YOUNG MIKE** *close and whispers something in his ear that we don't get to know.)*

(Almost definitely there's a moment when one of the **PLAYERS** *fucks up – drops a pass, shorts a route – and when it happens:)*

(The captains pull the team together and lead the **PLAYERS** *in push-ups...)*

(Which the team executes, in perfect unison...)

(Chanting, in perfect unison...)

(And springing back to their feet as one.)

(This happens every time a player fucks up in pre-game.)

(Every pre-game is a little bit different.)

(When the clock gets to about 1:30:)

*(***COACH*** gathers the* **PLAYERS** *together and leads them in prayer.)*

(Probably we don't hear this prayer.)

(There's something to their silence, the only sound on stage is **DAMON***'s intake of breath.)*

(And then silence.)

*(***COACH*** hands the team off to his captains...)*

(And **YOUNG MIKE** *and* **MARCUS** *lead them in a chant.)*

(One that starts softly but grows louder and louder...)

(And as **DAMON** *remains statue-still, the football* **PLAYERS** *work themselves into a frenzy...)*

(Erupting in a deafening, synchronized scream.)

(And when the clock strikes 0:00...)

(The lights drop to black.)

FIRST QUARTER

(With the stage dark, there is a rattling of drums...)

(Like the jingling of keys during an opening kick-off.)

(The rattling grows louder, and louder, and then silence...)

(As lights rise on **YOUNG MIKE** *and* **MARCUS***:)*

(Gazing skyward...)

(Awaiting the airborne kick-off.)

(When **MARCUS** *receives it:)*

(The clock ticks down from 15:00...)

(And a group of defenders rushes toward them.)

*(***YOUNG MIKE*** levels the first with a block...)*

(While **MARCUS** *jukes the second.)*

*(***YOUNG MIKE*** takes out a third, and* **MARCUS** *spins past a fourth.)*

(But a fifth defender wraps his arms around **MARCUS**' *waist...)*

(Unable to bring **MARCUS** *down...)*

(But leaving him upright and vulnerable to a sixth and final defender...)

(Who sets his sights on taking **MARCUS** *out.)*

*(***YOUNG MIKE*** sees this happen.)*

(He sees that his teammate's about to be levelled.)

(And his eyes go wide.)

(He explodes at the defender, driving at him like a sprinter bursting out of the blocks...)

(Then launches himself head-first – reckless, fearless.)

(But just before he connects...)

(Everything freezes.)

(Beat.)

(And **MIKE** *enters...)*

(Using a wheelchair...)

(Holding a remote control.)

(The lights transform to the flickering glow of a television screen...)

(As **MIKE** *wheels himself through the frozen scene of the* **PLAYERS***...)*

(Taking in everyone...)

(But settling near **MARCUS***.)*

(Beat.)

*(***MIKE** *presses a button on the remote...)*

(And the scene rewinds...)

(Back to **MARCUS**' *spin move.)*

*(***MIKE** *presses pause.)*

(Beat.)

(Then slow-motion forward.)

(And this time, when **MARCUS** *spins past his defender, there's an element of dance to his movement.)*

*(***MIKE** *presses pause...)*

(Then rewinds and watches the moment again.)

(And again, we see **MARCUS**' *spin move through* **MIKE**'*s eyes, and this time the dance is even more exaggerated and beautiful.)*

(*MIKE presses pause.*)

(*Right at that critical moment of recognition...*)

(*When* MARCUS *is wrapped up and vulnerable...*)

(*When* YOUNG MIKE *sees that his teammate is about to be levelled.*)

(MIKE *examines* MARCUS, *who looks truly helpless...*)

(*His arms pinned at his side, his body splayed open, looking to* YOUNG MIKE *and pleading for help.*)

(*Beat.*)

(MIKE *presses play, and* YOUNG MIKE *drives at the defender...*)

(*And when he connects...*)

(*Everything freezes, and lights burst to a full, natural light.*)

MIKE. You see what happened there?

PLAYERS. Yes sir!

COACH. (*Entering.*) He asked you a question--Did you see what happened?

PLAYERS. YES SIR!

> (*The* PLAYERS *snap off their helmets and drop to their knees.* YOUNG MIKE *and the* DEFENDER *remain frozen in place.*)

MIKE. (*To* PLAYERS.) There's a difference between fearless and reckless.

> (*Beat.*)

I left my feet, I led with my head--Make no mistake gentlemen...

What happened to me was no one's fault but my own.

> (*Beat.*)

MIKE. You play the right way you're gonna be fine.

COACH. Any questions?

PLAYERS. NO SIR!

COACH. Get outta here go lift some weights.

> *(The **PLAYERS** exit, one by one, and one by one they touch **MIKE** as they go.)*
>
> *(Maybe it's a fist bump.)*
>
> *(Maybe a shoulder tap – whatever it is, none of these **PLAYERS** look **MIKE** in the eye, and it's a bit unclear whether he's these boys' hero, their good luck charm, or the physical embodiment of their worst fear.)*
>
> *(We get to the last young man, and it's not a player, but **MIKE**'s younger self.)*
>
> *(When did he get out of his frozen position?)*
>
> *(How did we miss that?)*
>
> *(**YOUNG MIKE** looks his older self dead in the eyes and offers his fist for a bump.)*
>
> *(The older **MIKE** just stares at him.)*

*(To **MIKE**.)* How ya doin' Mike you okay?

> *(**YOUNG MIKE** throws **MIKE** a sarcastic look.)*

How's the rehab goin' it's goin' all right?

YOUNG MIKE. How is the rehab going?

MIKE. *(Turns his attention to **COACH**.)* It's a good group.

COACH. It's a good class they're good young men.

MIKE. They listen.

COACH. They listen to *you*. Tomorrow it's the sexual harassment guy, so...

MIKE. Yeah, good luck.

> *(They share a quiet laugh.)*

COACH. You um...

> *(Beat.)*

You good on money?

(MIKE nods.)

They haven't been sending you any bills have they?

(MIKE shakes his head.)

(COACH nods.)

(Beat.)

I should um...

MIKE. Yeah.

YOUNG MIKE. Ask him.

(Quick beat.)

COACH. It's good to see you, Mike.

YOUNG MIKE. Ask him.

(COACH starts to exit.)

Ask him.

MIKE. Hey, Coach?

(COACH stops and turns as MIKE turns to face him.)

I was just...

(Beat.)

No I was just wondering if you'd heard from Marcus.

COACH. *(Inhales, deeply uncomfortable.)* Oh, Mike, um...

MIKE. No I'm not--I was just wondering if you're still in touch.

(Beat.)

COACH. Yes I am.

MIKE & YOUNG MIKE. How is he?

(Beat.)

COACH. He's good he's real good he made the practice squad in Jacksonville, so...

(Beat.)

MIKE. Good.

(Quick beat.)

MIKE. Good that's good.

COACH. I better...

MIKE. Yeah.

COACH. They don't lift as hard when I'm not watchin'.

MIKE. No?

> *(Quick beat.)*

COACH. They're not all like you and Marcus.

MARCUS. *(Entering, as **COACH** exits.)* "And that's why they're captains, gentlemen."

YOUNG MIKE. *(With a grin.)* Jesus...

MARCUS. *(Imitating **COACH**.)* "They know that showin' up early is showin' up on time--"

YOUNG MIKE. *(Like, "enough.")* All right--

MARCUS. "--And showin' up on time is showin' up *late*."

YOUNG MIKE. You got a lotta energy at six a.m.

MARCUS. Bitch I had yoga at four-thirty.

> *(Off **YOUNG MIKE**'s look.)*

Oh don't even I'll do ballet if it keeps the swelling down. Check this out.

> *(**MARCUS** does a yoga pose for **YOUNG MIKE**.)*
>
> *(He's not exactly great.)*

YOUNG MIKE. You're doing it wrong.

MARCUS. Fuck you I'm making this look goo--

> *(**YOUNG MIKE** does it perfectly.)*
>
> *(**MARCUS** just looks at him.)*
>
> *(Beat.)*

YOUNG MIKE. What?

> *(Quick beat.)*

MARCUS. So, like um...

> *(**MARCUS** tries to imitate **YOUNG MIKE**'s pose.)*
>
> *(**YOUNG MIKE** comes out of his pose.)*

(He approaches **MARCUS**.*)*

(He adjusts **MARCUS**' *body.)*

(A dangerous moment passes between them.)

(And then – the sound of the team about to enter the gym.)

(And the temperature of the room instantly shifts, as **YOUNG MIKE** *and* **MARCUS** *snap into "Captain Mode.")*

(Barking at the **PLAYERS**.*)* Let's go let's go let's go--

YOUNG MIKE. Weight training starts at six a.m.--

MARCUS. *(As the* **PLAYERS** *enter.)* And showin' up on time is showin' up *late*--Oh I know you didn't just roll your eyes at me--

YOUNG MIKE. *(Barking at the* **PLAYERS**.*)* You better move your ass.

MARCUS. If one of us shows up late we *all* show up late--

YOUNG MIKE. You got five seconds to get your ass ready-- *Let's go.*

(Bodies should be moving, drums should be beating.)

(And when lights drop to black, then burst back up impossibly fast...)

(The team is training in perfect, percussive rhythm.)

PLAYERS. ONE!

(There's a **PLAYER** *benching on one part of the stage...)*

TWO!

(Another doing a power clean...)

THREE!

(Another doing a deadlift...)

FOUR!

(And downstage center...)

PLAYERS. FIVE!

>> *(There's **YOUNG MIKE**, squatting...)*

SIX!

>> *(**MARCUS** is spotting him...)*

SEVEN!

>> *(And a crowd of **PLAYERS** surrounds them both.)*

EIGHT!

MARCUS. I'm not helpin'--I'm not even helpin'.

PLAYERS. NINE!

MARCUS. This is all you--I'm not helpin'--I'm not helpin' this is all you--*C'mon.*

PLAYERS.

>> TEN!   *(**YOUNG MIKE** yells as he puts it up.)*

>> *(The yell sustains.)*

>> *(It's a battle cry – complete release – and when the scream comes to an abrupt stop...)*

>> *(The stage fucking shakes.)*

YOUNG MIKE. Who's the bitch now, huh? Who's the fucking bitch?!

MARCUS. All right all right--

YOUNG MIKE. Who's the fucking pussy ass bitch now?!

MARCUS. Aight Jesus step back.

>> *(Moving into position.)*

God-damn.

>> *(As he sets himself.)*

I gotta do ten?

YOUNG MIKE. Try eleven.

MARCUS. Bitch you did ten.

YOUNG MIKE. You playing to tie?

PLAYERS. *(Ad-lib.)* Awww...

MARCUS. *(To* **YOUNG MIKE***.)* You help me up?

>*(Quick beat.)*

YOUNG MIKE. *(Absolute loyalty.)* I got you.

>(**MARCUS** *takes a few sharp intakes of breath, as a few of the* **PLAYERS** *shout, "C'mon, Marcus, c'mon," and "Receiver pride, baby, receiver pride.")*

Three...

>*(Quick beat.)*

MARCUS. Two...

>*(Quick beat.)*

YOUNG MIKE & MARCUS. *One.*

YOUNG MIKE. You got this--*C'mon.*

>(**MARCUS** *does the first rep with a grunt.)*

PLAYERS. *ONE!*

>*(Beat.)*

TWO!

>*(Beat.)*

THREE!

>*(Blackout.)*

FOUR!

>*(Beat.)*

FIVE!

>*(Beat.)*

SIX!

>*(Beat.)*

SEVEN!

>*(Beat.)*

EIGHT!

>*(Beat.)*

NINE!

> *(Beat.)*

TEN!

> *(Beat.)*

JERRY. Eleven.

> *(Lights rise...)*

Twelve.

> *(And we're at **MIKE**'s physical therapy.)*

Thirteen.

> *(**MIKE**'s doing TKE's [Terminal Knee Extensions], extending his leg, over and over again.)*

You do know you were supposed to stop at ten.

> *(**MIKE** does a couple more...)*
>
> *(Then stops, completely exhausted.)*
>
> *(**JERRY** touches him on the chest...)*

Nice work.

> *(But **MIKE** knocks **JERRY**'s hand away as soon as he's touched.)*

Well...you're a bit feisty.

> *(No response.)*

Maybe it's a good day to finally do one of those dreaded sit-to-stands.

MIKE. I'm not feelin' the sit-to-stands today.

JERRY. You weren't feeling 'em yesterday, either.

MIKE. And you said that was fine.

JERRY. Yesterday you didn't show up late.

MIKE. I *told* you I was going to be late--

JERRY.	**MIKE.**
And I told you--	I *told* you--

JERRY. --That was a problem.

MIKE. Look I was doing a safety training, if you must know--

JERRY. I didn't ask--

MIKE. What, you want more people to end up like me?

JERRY.	**MIKE.**
Why do you use the phrase, *end up*--	Oh, or is that your game--

MIKE. --You're trying to build yourself a whole client base of football players like me.

JERRY. I *have* a client base of football players.

> *(Beat.)*

And most of them don't want to do sit-to-stands, either. And I get it, your legs used to work in a way--

JERRY.	**MIKE.**
The rest of us can only imagine--	All right, okay...

JERRY. I remember, I was at this game, right here at the university--

MIKE. Time's up.

JERRY. Time's up when I say it's up.

> *(Quick beat.)*

So we've got the ball on our own one-yard line. And common sense says quarterback sneak, right, give the offense some space to work with.

But we pitch it, to this...*undersized* tailback.

> (**MIKE** *looks at* **JERRY**.)

> (**YOUNG MIKE** *enters*.)

And the defense, they've been assuming sneak, too, so when we snap the ball, they collapse at the line and the tailback...

He just flies right past 'em.

> (**YOUNG MIKE** *slowly approaches* **MIKE**.)

So now there's just two men to beat--The safety and the corner--That's it.

The safety's first and our tailback does this spin move and it's not football it's *dance*.

(**YOUNG MIKE** *stands behind* **JERRY** – *so that* **MIKE** *can look at both of them.*)

But that is nothing compared to what happens next.

(**YOUNG MIKE** *grins.*)

And there's a part of me, sitting up there in the stands-- because I'm a graduate of the sports medicine program at the University of Texas--I should be able to *account* for what happens next.

(**YOUNG MIKE** *looks at* **MIKE** *with a question:* "*Do you want to see this?*")

I *should* be able to say, "Well this man's muscles twitch at a higher velocity--That's why he can do this."--But I am every bit as convinced as everyone else...

That what I'm watching is impossible.

(**MIKE** *nods,* "*Yes.*")

'Cause our tailback, he turns on a--No, he doesn't turn on a dime--He turns on a pinpoint. He is going twenty miles per hour in one direction and then suddenly...

(*And then it happens.*)

(**YOUNG MIKE** *flies.*)

He is still.

(*Quick beat.*)

And a hundred thousand people go quiet...
As everything in front of our tailback just...
Opens up.

(**YOUNG MIKE** *walks the length of the stage, simply and freely...*)

(*As the scoreboard lights up with seven points.*)

What I'm saying is this.

When you've set the record for the longest run in the history of college football--When you have stunned a city's worth of screaming fans into silence.

Well I get that it's insulting, when I want to strap you into a belt...

So I can help you stand...

So you can take the first step toward taking five steps with the assistance of a walker.

(Quick beat.)

But I don't give a shit if you're insulted.

*(**MIKE** looks at **JERRY**, as **DAMON** appears in the doorway.)*

Your body is atrophying. And you only have so much time to save it.

*(**MIKE** looks away.)*

If the clock runs out and you haven't found a way to move forward, you never will.

DAMON. I'm...

I'm sorry they...

They said I could just come on back.

I can...

MIKE. It's fine, Dad, it's fine.

*(Looks at **JERRY**.)*

We were done here, anyway, isn't that right?

*(**DAMON** gets behind **MIKE** to push him, but then:)*

YOUNG MIKE. He left out the best part of the story.

*(**JERRY** and **DAMON** enter a soft freeze as:)*

*(To **JERRY**.)* It wasn't when I ran ninety-nine yards, un-fucking-touched.

*(To **MIKE**.)*

And it wasn't when I crossed the goal line.

MIKE. It was the moment after.

YOUNG MIKE. When I turned around...

(**MARCUS** *enters.*)

And the first person I saw...

(**MARCUS** *approaches* **YOUNG MIKE.**)

(*And then:*)

(*They perform a touchdown celebration dance in perfect sync.*)

(*It probably starts with a little swagger [dusting off the shoulders, etc.].*)

(*But it evolves into something intimate – maybe an embrace, maybe a lift.*)

(*That moment of intense physical connection that football permits.*)

And *that*...

(*Turns to* **JERRY.**)

That's a fucking dance.

JERRY. (*Comes out of freeze.*) You'll think about what I said, Mike.

(**MIKE** *inhales deeply, keeping this all in.*)

(*Before he can exhale,* **DAMON** *pushes him offstage.*)

(**JERRY** *rubs his eyes, inhales deeply...*)

(*And without exhaling, exits offstage.*)

(**YOUNG MIKE** *watches him go...*)

(*Then turns and looks at the game clock...*)

(*And watches as the final seconds of the first quarter tick down.*)

(*Lights fade...*)

SECOND QUARTER

(...Then rise on **DAMON** *pushing* **MIKE** *into their home.)*

(The clock ticks down from 15:00.)

DAMON. I picked some things up from the grocery store if you're hungry.

*(**MIKE** nods; Quick beat.)*

Are you...are you hungry?

*(**MIKE** shakes his head.)*

I could make you a sandwich or--

MIKE. Dad I've been out of the hospital for six months--

DAMON. I know I--

MIKE. If I'm hungry I can make something myself.

DAMON. I know you can I...

(Quick beat.)

Of course you can I--

MIKE. I'm just tired okay I just want to get some sleep.

(Beat.)

DAMON. Sure.

(Quick beat.)

Sure I'll just go get your pjs.

MIKE. They're *not*...

DAMON. I didn't mean... I'm sorry I--

MIKE. No *I'm* sorry I...

(Quick beat.)

I appreciate your getting them thank you.

(Beat.)

(**DAMON** *nods, exits.*)

(**MIKE** *watches him go...*)

(*Then, once alone...*)

(*Makes an effort to push himself to standing.*)

(*He gets a few inches off his chair...*)

(*When* **YOUNG MIKE** *enters, watching him.*)

(*Beat.*)

YOUNG MIKE. Your arms are shaking.

(*Beat.*)

You want some help?

(*He moves to* **MIKE.**)

MIKE. Don't.

(**YOUNG MIKE** *chuckles, then:*)

YOUNG MIKE. Not even a finger?

MIKE. Don't fucking touch me.

YOUNG MIKE. Oooh--What happened to *you*? I never minded being touched.

(**MIKE** *looks at* **YOUNG MIKE**...)

(*As* **YOUNG MIKE** *uses his one finger to push* **MIKE** *back down.*)

(*The two share a look and hold it.*)

God you look old.

(*Quick beat.*)

It's been ten months you look like you've aged ten years.

(**DAMON** *enters with a basket of laundry.*)

DAMON. I wasn't quite sure what you wanted to wear, so...

YOUNG MIKE. (*Spotting something in the laundry.*) Oh no fucking way.

(*He snags a T-shirt out of the basket, while* **DAMON** *pulls out another T-shirt.*)

You still have this?

DAMON. Is this all right?

YOUNG MIKE. Well hello, favorite shirt.

>(**YOUNG MIKE** *pulls off the shirt he's wearing...*)
>
>(*And catches* **MIKE** *looking at his body.*)

Nice, right?

DAMON. Let me help you.

>(**DAMON** *goes to help* **MIKE** *change his shirt.*)

MIKE. *(Sharply.)* I got it.

>(**MIKE** *takes off his shirt.*)
>
>(**YOUNG MIKE** *looks at him. He doesn't say a word about the difference between their bodies.*)
>
>(*He doesn't have to.*)
>
>(**MIKE** *goes to put on the new shirt...*)
>
>(*But the back of his shirt gets caught on the handle of his chair.*)
>
>(**DAMON** *moves to help him.*)
>
>(*And notices a possible pressure sore on his son's back.*)

What's wrong?

DAMON. It's noth...

>(**DAMON** *clears his throat, and then – behind his back and unseen by* **MIKE** *– does a little movement with his hand.*)
>
>(*Just something small to let out a little frustration and pain.*)

It's fine it's just a rash I'll go get some ointment I'll be right back.

>(**DAMON** *exits.*)
>
>(*And there's a silence between* **MIKE** *and* **YOUNG MIKE.**)
>
>(**YOUNG MIKE** *tugs his own T-shirt.*)

YOUNG MIKE. *(Softly.)* Still has the grass stain.

> *(Quick beat.)*
>
> (**MIKE** *nods.*)
>
> *(Quick beat.)*

You um...

MIKE. Yeah.

YOUNG MIKE. You remember how pissed he got?

> *(Beat.)*

MIKE. Yeah.

> *(Lights shift [and perhaps there's the blast of a drum] as* **DAMON** *bursts through the door.)*

DAMON. MICHAEL SHAW WHERE HAVE YOU BEEN?!

YOUNG MIKE. Jesus scream a little louder I don't think the entire neighborhood--

DAMON. Where were you this afternoon?!

YOUNG MIKE. I told you where I was gonna be--

DAMON. And I told *you* that was not allowed.

YOUNG MIKE. Yeah, well, tryouts aren't exactly optional.

DAMON. Neither is rehearsal.

> *(Quick beat.)*

You choose right now how you're gonna spend your time.

YOUNG MIKE. Dad...

DAMON. No you decide right *now*...

Whether you're gonna take a lifetime of training and throw it away--You choose now:

The company or this team.

> *(Beat.)*

JERRY. So why football?

> *(And we're back in one of* **MIKE**'s *physical therapy appointments.)*

Why'd you choose football? Other hand.

(MIKE's working a TheraBand, or weights...)

Did you grow up with it?

(While JERRY assists. It's a rigorous workout.)

Did you grow up watching it?

(MIKE smirks to himself.)

Is something funny?

MIKE. You seriously talk more than any person I've ever met.

JERRY. I'm trying to put the therapist back into physical therapy.

(Quick beat.)

You're welcome to go the more traditional route--I'd be happy to set you up with a physical therapist, an occupational therapist, and a psychologist.

Or you can have me. One-stop shopping--Three degrees, all in one.

(Quick beat.)

MIKE. Not all.

JERRY. I'm sorry?

MIKE. I've got the sex education guy tomorrow, so...

JERRY. Ooh.

MIKE. Yeah.

JERRY. Good luck.

(They share a half-laugh.)

Hey if he tries to tell you that hugging is just as good as sex, punch him in the dick, all right?

(And this time they share a real laugh. A quiet one, sure, but it's the first time MIKE's guard has come down with JERRY – even a little.)

You *are* gonna have sex again at some point--You know that, right?

(MIKE looks away...)

(*As lights rise on...*)

(**YOUNG MIKE**, *shirtless, in boxers, talking to someone offstage.*)

YOUNG MIKE. Will you just come out of there?

MIKE. (*To* **YOUNG MIKE**, *to the memory.*) No.

JERRY. You will, Mike.

MIKE. (*To* **JERRY**.) Can we talk about something else?

(*Lights fade on* **YOUNG MIKE**.)

JERRY. Was it a daddy thing?

MIKE. *What?*

JERRY. The reason you chose football.

MIKE. Nice transition.

JERRY. Did he pressure you into playing?

(*Off* **MIKE***'s smirk.*)

I'm sorry I don't understand the joke.

MIKE. My father's Damon Shaw.

(*Lights rise on* **DAMON**, *perhaps in shadow, warming up for rehearsal.*)

(*Trying to get those old bones and muscles loose.*)

As in the Damon Shaw Dance Company?

JERRY. I'm sorry I'm not much of a dance fan.

MIKE. Wow I pegged that one wrong.

JERRY. Oh I see because I'm gay I must love dance.

MIKE. I hate to break it to you, but most of our audience was gay.

JERRY. (*Realizing.*) You were in the company.

(*Quick beat.*)

Well--Switch hands--Your father must have loved it when you started playing football.

MIKE. Only son in the history of the United States to disappoint his dad by choosing football over dance.

(*Quick beat.*)

JERRY. You're like the opposite of Billy Elliot.

> *(Beat.)*

So why football?

> *(**MIKE** looks at **JERRY**.)*

Why'd you choose football?

BOY #1. Hey Billy Elliot!

> *(Lights crossfade to **YOUNG MIKE**, wearing headphones...)*
>
> *(And being trailed by a crowd of **BOYS**.)*

BOY #2. Hey! Hey fuckhead! HEY!

> *(**YOUNG MIKE** turns and faces the crowd of **BOYS**.)*

BOY #3. You think maybe you could tap dance off the field?

> *(**YOUNG MIKE** removes the headphones.)*

We're trying to play a game here.

YOUNG MIKE. Oh. Oh sorry I...

I just sometimes I run choreography in my head and I totally forget where I am.

> *(Quick beat.)*

BOY #4. The fuck did he just say?

> *(**BOY #5** walks up to **YOUNG MIKE** and pulls him aside.)*

BOY #5. Look dude I'm gonna tell you somethin' 'cause I like you 'cause you let me cheat off you in geometry but you talk like that you're gonna get your ass kicked.

YOUNG MIKE. Yeah, okay...

BOY #5. No, seriously, you--

BOY #6. GET OFF--

BOY #7. THE FUCKING--

BOY #8. FIELD.

> *(Beat.)*

YOUNG MIKE. *(To* **BOY #5**.*)* You're not gonna say anything?

(BOY #5 is silent.)

YOUNG MIKE. Fine.

(YOUNG MIKE starts to exit.)

BOY #8. There ya go.

BOY #7. Run home to Daddy.

BOY #6. You fucking fairy--

BOY #4. He's got some tights for you to try on.

(YOUNG MIKE spins back around.)

YOUNG MIKE. Oh dude whatever--*You* wear tights.

BOY #5. Hey--don't.

BOY #3. What did you just say--

BOY #5. Don't, okay? It's not worth it--

YOUNG MIKE. And you're calling *me* a fairy? You guys celebrate by grabbing each other's ass.

BOY #2. All right motherfucker.

BOY #5. Hey--Whoa whoa--Hey--Easy hey--

(Getting in between.)

We need you on Friday--

(BOY #2 doesn't desist.)

Hey settle it on the field, okay?

(BOY #2 stops.)

We'll have him run the gauntlet, okay?

(BOY #2 grins.)

All right?

(Beat.)

BOY #2. Shirts.

(And with just that little prompting, all the **BOYS** *remove their shirts.)*

(They place their shirts into two lines – like sidelines on a football field.)

(YOUNG MIKE watches in silence, and then looks at all the shirtless men.)

YOUNG MIKE. Yeah you're right; this is way less gay.

BOY #2. Let's go--*Right now.*

YOUNG MIKE. Excuse me?

BOY #5. You have to get from there...

> *(Points to one end of the field.)*

To there...

> *(Points to the other end.)*

Only thing standing in your way...

BOY #2. Let's fucking go.

BOY #5. *(To* **YOUNG MIKE**, *softer.)* Look you can do it this way...or we will beat the shit out of you right now.

> *(**BOY #2** shoves a football into **YOUNG MIKE**'s gut.)*

> *(Rejoining the **BOYS**.)*

He starts moving when you start moving.

> *(And maybe we see **DAMON** dancing in shadow...)*

> *(We get to see his influence on his son.)*

> *(Because when **BOY #2** breaks at **YOUNG MIKE**, full-tilt, running to knock his head off...)*

> *(**YOUNG MIKE** instinctively does a pirouette...)*

> *(And **BOY #2** flies right by him.)*

> *(Everyone is stunned for just a moment...)*

> *(And then:)*

BOY #2. AGAIN!

YOUNG MIKE. What? No--Hey--We did the stupid--

BOY #2. *(Slapping the floor.)* AGAIN!

> *(**YOUNG MIKE** inhales, and this time, he choreographs his path.)*

> *(And when **BOY #2** charges at him, diving at his knees, **YOUNG MIKE** leaps over him, basically doing the splits in mid-air.)*

YOUNG MIKE. JETÉ!

> *(Then; gaining confidence.)*

One more time?

> *(**BOY #2** charges him.)*

Maybe we'll do something hip-hop--

> *(**YOUNG MIKE** jukes **BOY #2**, who crumbles at the ankles.)*

Oooh...

> *(**YOUNG MIKE** moonwalks/b-boys in victory, looking at **BOY #2**, taunting him...)*
>
> *(But altogether oblivious to **BOY #1**, who steps into the gauntlet, and runs full-tilt at **YOUNG MIKE**.)*
>
> *(And just as their bodies connect...)*
>
> *(The lights drop, immediately rising on:)*

COACH. *(Facing out.)* Listen up gentlemen we're gonna have a little talk and we're gonna *have* a little talk--

COACH.	**MIKE.**
--'Cause you've all forgotten what it was like the first time you got hit.	Listen up gentlemen we're gonna have a little talk and we're gonna *have* a little talk--

MIKE. 'Cause you've all forgotten what it was like the first time you got hit.

> *(Lights re-rise on **YOUNG MIKE** and **BOY #1**, frozen in the moment after collision.)*

COACH. I want you to think back--

MIKE. I want you to remember--

COACH. That first time you got hit--

MIKE. I mean *really* hit--

COACH. 'Cause you and I know--

COACH & MIKE. There is nothing good about it.

*(Lights rise on **DAMON** in a separate space, facing out.)*

DAMON. What did you just say?

COACH. Bone striking bone.

DAMON. You want to try out for *what*?

COACH. And then that flash--

MIKE. That split second--

COACH & MIKE. Everything goes *white*.

DAMON. Well of course I'm upset--

MIKE. And for a moment you think--

DAMON & COACH. Our bodies are not made for this.

DAMON. Your body is a vehicle for language.

COACH & MIKE. Most people get hit that first time--

DAMON. Most people never speak with their bodies--

MIKE. They walk away--

DAMON. They're stuck to *this*.

(Slams his hand to his throat.)

MIKE. They give up--

DAMON. You will give up this idea right here right now.

COACH. But you made a choice--

DAMON. Because if you choose to *silence* your body...

COACH. You made a choice--

DAMON. I will never speak to you again.

MIKE. *(Firm.)* You made a choice.

YOUNG MIKE. This is such...*bullshit*.

*(**YOUNG MIKE** rises out of the tackle and moves to **MIKE** while the rest of the stage stays still.)*

*(To **MIKE**.)* "There is nothing good about it"?

MIKE. I'm not saying anything that isn't true--

YOUNG MIKE. No fuck you--You wanna take their money? Fine.

You wanna promise not to sue 'em? Do these bullshit safety trainings say the same goddamned things Coach used to say?

Fine.

> (**YOUNG MIKE** *walks to his father.*)

(To **DAMON**.*)* But you listen to me.
That first time I got hit?

> (**DAMON** *turns and looks at* **YOUNG MIKE**.*)

I liked it.

MIKE. It hurt like fucking hell.

YOUNG MIKE. *(Turns to* **MIKE**.*)* That split-second.

MIKE. That flash.

YOUNG MIKE. Everything goes white.

MIKE. And for a second--

YOUNG MIKE. You think--

MIKE. I am dead.

> *(Beat.)*

YOUNG MIKE. But then...

> *(Quick beat.)*

MIKE. *(Admitting.)* You open your eyes.

YOUNG MIKE. And Jesus Christ--

MIKE. Oh my god--

YOUNG MIKE & MIKE. I AM ALIVE.

> *(Quick beat.)*

YOUNG MIKE. *(To* **DAMON**.*)* I'm alive.
Goddammit I'm alive and you look that guy in the eyes
and you tell him:

PLAYERS & YOUNG MIKE. YOU THINK YOU CAN HURT
ME?!

YOUNG MIKE. YOU CANNOT HURT ME.

> *(Beat.)*

You are *nothing* to me.

> *(Quick beat.)*

> (**DAMON** *exits...*)

> (As **MARCUS** *enters.*)

MARCUS. I bet *I* can hurt you.

> *(Beat.)*

COACH. Mike?

> *(Quick beat.)*

> *(**YOUNG MIKE** grins.)*

YOUNG MIKE. Do your best.

COACH. And that's why they're captains gentlemen.

> *(Re: **YOUNG MIKE**.)*

I want you to look at this young man right here. He could've gone pro last year.

He could be playing in the No Fun League right now.

> *(**YOUNG MIKE** approaches **MARCUS**...)*

I told you it would be worth it to come back, didn't I Mike?

MIKE. Yes sir.

COACH. Was I wrong?

YOUNG MIKE. *(Looking at **MARCUS**.)* No sir. This is exactly where I want to be.

COACH. Into position.

> *(**YOUNG MIKE** and **MARCUS** take a three-point stance.)*

> *(Their bodies are perfectly still, and perfectly sprung.)*

> *(And then:)*

HUT!

> *(**MARCUS** drives through **YOUNG MIKE**, lightning-fast, wrapping him up and taking him to the ground.)*

You see what happened there?

PLAYERS. Yes sir!

> *(**MARCUS** and **YOUNG MIKE** rise to their feet.)*

COACH. Again!

(They get into position.)

COACH. HUT!

(MARCUS does it again.)

You see what Mike did wrong?

PLAYERS. Yes sir!

(They rise to their feet.)

COACH. Again!

(They get into position...)

HUT!

(But this time, we see it in slow-motion...)

(And watch as MARCUS wraps his arms around YOUNG MIKE's body and buries his head in his chest.)

You see how Marcus got under those pads?

PLAYERS. YES SIR!

(MARCUS puts the full weight of his body into YOUNG MIKE, lifting him off the ground.)

(YOUNG MIKE closes his eyes, enjoying one of the rare embraces that he's allowed to experience with MARCUS.)

COACH. Do not let them underneath gentlemen you let them under that armor you *will* get hurt.

(And then silence...)

(As MARCUS lands on top of YOUNG MIKE.)

Felt good, didn't it Marcus?

(Quick beat.)

MARCUS. *(Terrified.)* Yes sir.

COACH. Hit someone the right way it's the greatest feeling in the world.

(MARCUS offers YOUNG MIKE his hand to lift him up.)

Do it right you don't feel any pain at all.

> *(A blast of drums and a flash of light.)*

YOUNG MIKE. *(Panicked.)* I can't feel...

I can't...

I can't feel my fucking legs!

MARCUS. *(Holding* **YOUNG MIKE**'s *hand.)* You're okay it's okay--

YOUNG MIKE. I CAN'T FEEL MY FUCKING LEGS!

MARCUS. It's just a stinger, baby, trainer's comin'--

YOUNG MIKE. *(Softer.)* Marcus I can't move my fucking--

MARCUS. Hey *hey*--You're gonna be fine, okay, you're *invincible.* Nothin' hurts you.

YOUNG MIKE. *(Softer.)* Just take my hand, okay, man?

> *(***MARCUS** *looks down; he's already holding it.)*

Will you just take my fuckin' hand?!

MIKE. I don't want to talk about this anymore.

> *(Lights rise on a session with* **JERRY** *and* **MIKE**.*)*

JERRY. There's just one thing--

MIKE.	**JERRY.**
I don't want to *talk*--	--I don't understand--

JERRY. You were taught how to tackle and block.

MIKE. Yeah, so?

JERRY. You were trained properly.

MIKE. What's your point?

JERRY. You didn't do it properly the day you got hurt.

> *(Quick beat.)*

You *launched* yourself at the defender--head-first. *Why?*

> *(Beat.)*

> *(***YOUNG MIKE** *rises, looks right at* **MARCUS**.*)*

> *(Beat.)*

YOUNG MIKE. *Tell him.*

> (**MIKE** *turns to* **YOUNG MIKE;** **YOUNG MIKE**
> *turns to him.*)

Go ahead.

> (**MIKE** *looks at the clock, which has nearly
> ticked down to zero.*)

MIKE. Time's up.

JERRY. Not quite.

YOUNG MIKE. I'm calling time-out.

> (*The clock freezes.*)

See; clock's frozen.

> (*Quick beat.*)

Tell him.

JERRY. Mike?

YOUNG MIKE. But tell him the truth. Don't tell him that
bullshit that blood money turncoat "There's a difference
between fearless and reckless--"

MIKE. The thing is--

YOUNG MIKE. Tell him the *truth.*

> (*Beat.*)

> (**MIKE** *stares at* **YOUNG MIKE.**)

MIKE. The thing is there's a difference between fearless--

YOUNG MIKE. Oh my god--

MIKE. And I was reckless--

YOUNG MIKE. You make me sick.

MIKE. I ignored my training--

YOUNG MIKE. This was supposed to be a--These people
paid to see a *contest.*

MIKE. It was no one's fault but my--

YOUNG MIKE. You're not even giving them a game.

> (*Lights shift.*)

MIKE. (*To* **YOUNG MIKE.**) I'm *trying.*

YOUNG MIKE. The fuck you are. Wh-what, with your little TheraBand exercises? I'd just as soon you stay home and jack off and save us all the trouble.

MIKE. Look FUCK YOU--

YOUNG MIKE. Oh right you can't jack off 'cause you can't get it up.

(Quick beat.)

You wanna feel me?

I'm hard right now--I am hard all over--I *break* my body to build it back; you won't even walk five goddamned feet with the assistance of a walker.

And you think your story can compete with mine?

(Quick beat.)

I denied a father. I risked my life. Every play every game--I fought for who I loved. And you?

(Quick beat.)

You won't even speak his name.

(Quick beat.)

You'd rather just sit at home and watch old videos of me. You think I'll ever watch a video of you? You think anyone wants to see how your story plays out?

(To audience.)

Go home.

I'm sorry we wasted your time.

I honestly thought he'd put up a fight.

(MIKE *watches* **YOUNG MIKE** *start to leave...)*

(And then turns to **JERRY.***)*

MIKE. I was in love with one of my teammates.

(YOUNG MIKE *stops.)*

He had the ball, and one of the players from the other team was about to hurt the man I loved.

(Beat.)

MIKE. And so I went at him, full-speed fearless and I left my feet and I led with my head...

(He turns to face **YOUNG MIKE.***)*

And I laid that motherfucker out.

(Beat.)

YOUNG MIKE. Well...

(The clock starts to tick down.)

Maybe we have a game after all.

(The clock hits 0:00. Blackout.)

HALFTIME

(And I'm beginning to think, more and more, that this play runs with no intermission.)

(That "Halftime" consists – as so many halftimes do – with a performance by a visiting group.)

(In this case, the visiting group happens to be the **DAMON SHAW DANCE COMPANY***...)*

(Back when **YOUNG MIKE** *was a part of it.)*

(What their performance looks like I don't fully know...)

(But the heart and soul of it should be a duet between **YOUNG MIKE** *and* **DAMON***.)*

(For just a moment, let us see the Mike that **DAMON** *sees when he looks at his son.)*

(And then the moment's gone.)

(Because Halftime's over.)

THIRD QUARTER

(The clock ticks down from 15:00 as...)

(Lights rise on **YOUNG MIKE***, wearing nothing but boxers.)*

(He looks offstage to a hallway we can't see...)

(Then goes to dim down the lights.)

(He paces, cracking his knuckles, taking a breath in without taking one out, then goes to check himself in a mirror.)

(Not satisfied with what he sees, he drops to the floor and does twenty push-ups, lightning-fast.)

(He pops back up, checks himself out, flicks his nipples, grabs his package to make sure he's hard.)

(He cracks his knuckles, waiting, nervous.)

(Another breath in without one out.)

(Finally...)

YOUNG MIKE. Will you just come out of there?

(A sliver of light slices across the stage as an offstage door to an offstage bathroom opens and shuts.)

*(***MARCUS** *enters, fully-clothed.)*

(Beat.)

You're um...

(Quick beat.)

You're dressed.

MARCUS. Yeah look I'm just gonna bounce, aight?

YOUNG MIKE. *(Softly.) What?*

MARCUS. All the fellas at the club, so...

YOUNG MIKE. Wha...

> *(Quick beat.)*

Why are y...

MARCUS. *(Like, "What's the big deal?")* What?

YOUNG MIKE. *(Mocking his "thug" effect.)* All the fellas at the club...

MARCUS. Jesus.

YOUNG MIKE.	**MARCUS.**
Why are you...	I'm sorry...

MARCUS. *(Mock intellectual tone.)* All of our teammates have fled their hotel room under the cover of darkness.

YOUNG MIKE. Why are you doing this?

MARCUS. You can come with if you want.

YOUNG MIKE. To the strip club.

MARCUS. Yeah.

YOUNG MIKE. I'm not going to the strip club.

MARCUS. Aight, Jesus--

YOUNG MIKE. You think I want to go to the fucking strip club?

MARCUS. I's just askin'--

YOUNG MIKE. They probably can't even fucking dance.

> *(Quick beat.)*

MARCUS. *What?*

YOUNG MIKE. The strippers; I bet they can't dance for shit.

MARCUS. Jesus Chri--See this is why--

YOUNG MIKE. I'm just saying, it's insulting.

MARCUS. NO ONE'S GOING THERE TO WATCH THEM DANCE.

YOUNG MIKE. Yeah, why are you going?

> *(Beat.)*

MARCUS. *(Softer.)* Man what the fuck you think they're gonna say we're the only ones not there?

YOUNG MIKE. They're gonna say exactly what we told them--

> *(MARCUS breathes in.)*

That we're the captains of this team and captains can't get caught at a strip club.

MARCUS. And no one's gonna notice we're sharin' a room.

YOUNG MIKE. That's what teammates do--I mean Jesus we been talkin' 'bout this for weeks we been plannin' this out for--

MARCUS. No you been plannin' it I just said we share a hotel room and you had to turn into a fuckin' bitch and...

> *(Stops himself.)*
>
> *(Beat.)*

YOUNG MIKE. So go then.

MARCUS. Jesus Mike I--

YOUNG MIKE. No fuck you, all right?

> *(Quick beat.)*

I *have* been looking forward to this for weeks, but if that's where you wanna be, go. If here's where you wanna be, stay.

But if you're not willing to be where you wanna be, then there's a bitch in this room and it's not me.

> *(Beat.)*

MARCUS. *(Breathes in.)* Door locked?

> *(YOUNG MIKE nods.)*
>
> *(Beat.)*
>
> *(YOUNG MIKE breathes in.)*
>
> *(Beat.)*

YOUNG MIKE. I feel like we're supposed to do something now.

MARCUS. Right? I half expect Coach to be like, "You see gentlemen, you see how he gently removes his boxers?"

> *(The two quietly laugh.)*
>
> *(Then...)*

What?

> *(Quick beat.)*

YOUNG MIKE. You want to take off my boxers?

> *(Beat.)*

MARCUS. Turn off the lights.

> *(Beat.)*
>
> *(**YOUNG MIKE** goes and turns off the lights.)*
>
> *(The men are just silhouettes in the darkness.)*
>
> *(**YOUNG MIKE** comes to **MARCUS**, and under the cover of darkness, the two begin to cautiously, clumsily, explore each other's bodies.)*
>
> *(There's no sound but a few sharp breaths in.)*

JERRY. Did you ever tell anyone?

> *(Lights rise on **MIKE** and **JERRY**.)*

You ever tell your father?

YOUNG MIKE. Don't.

JERRY. Mike?

YOUNG MIKE. I'll take a time-out, whatever, just...

YOUNG MIKE & MIKE. Just give me a second, okay?

YOUNG MIKE. I just want to stay *here*.

> *(Quick beat.)*

JERRY. It just seems like your father would've been supportive.

> *(No response.)*

Of course you and your father weren't speaking at the time. Because the last time you opened up to him he shut you out.

MIKE. Jesus Christ...

JERRY. It seems *every* time you open up to another man--

MIKE. Can you not--

JERRY. The last man you opened up to--

> (**MARCUS** *exits.*)

MIKE & YOUNG MIKE. Just *don't*, okay?

JERRY. Is *this* why you won't do a sit-to-stand? It's not 'cause it feels insulting.

MIKE. It *is* insulting.

JERRY. I have to strap you into a belt; I have to *hold* you.

MIKE. Oh my fucking God--

JERRY. The last man who held you--

MIKE. If I do the sit-to-stand will you drop the psycho-analytical bullshit?

> (*Beat.*)

YOUNG MIKE. You sure you want to do this?

> (*Quick beat.*)

JERRY. All right.

> (*Quick beat.*)

YOUNG MIKE. All right.

JERRY. Lean forward.

YOUNG MIKE. But I hope you're ready.

JERRY. Mike?

YOUNG MIKE. 'Cause I've kept you in the game till now...

> (**MIKE** *starts to lean forward;* **YOUNG MIKE** *holds him back.*)

But when I'm through with you you're going to *live* in the past.

> (**MIKE** *brushes* **YOUNG MIKE**'s *hand away and leans forward.*)
>
> (*But when* **JERRY** *unravels a belt...*)

COACH. Let's go gentlemen...

(**COACH** *enters, trailed by the* **PLAYERS**.)

YOUNG MIKE. You see?

(*Half the* **PLAYERS** *unravel bungee cords.*)

You see?

(**MARCUS** *unravels a bungee cord.*)

The harder you try to move forward, the more you can't help but go back.

(**MARCUS** *wraps the bungee cord around* **YOUNG MIKE**'s *waist, as* **JERRY** *wraps the belt around* **MIKE**'s *waist.*)

JERRY & MARCUS. Too tight?

YOUNG MIKE & MIKE. No.

(*The* **PLAYERS** *gather on one "side of the field."*)

JERRY. Now listen to me Mike--

COACH. Half of you can barely stand--

JERRY. You probably won't stand the first time--

COACH. Your legs are *shot*--

JERRY. As soon as you rise up--

COACH. Your lungs are burning--

JERRY. Your blood pressure will drop.

COACH. You just want this to be over--

JERRY. We'll stop when you tell me--

COACH. Only when our bodies are *broken* does our work begin.

(*Quick beat.*)

JERRY. You ready?

COACH. Into position.

(*Half the* **PLAYERS**, *including* **YOUNG MIKE**, *position themselves in a line. They have the bungee cords wrapped around their waists.*)

(*The other half are directly behind them, holding the cords, offering resistance, trying to hold them back.*)

(**JERRY** *gets into position to help* **MIKE** *rise.*)

JERRY. On your count, okay?

COACH. Call it off, Mike.

MIKE. Three...

YOUNG MIKE. Breakdown!

(*The* **PLAYERS** *snap into starting position.*)

MIKE. TWO...

YOUNG MIKE. DOWN, SET...

MIKE. *ONE...*

COACH. *HUT!!*

(*The snares snap like a starter gun...*)

(*And the* **PLAYERS** *shoot like sprinters out of the gates...*)

(*As* **MIKE** *rises, just inches off his chair.*)

(*The* **PLAYERS** *move slower and slower as the resistance gets stronger and stronger...*)

(*The movement nearly stopping as the* **PLAYERS** *struggle to drive forward.*)

(*And* **MIKE** *and* **JERRY** *struggle to rise up.*)

This is where the training comes in, gentlemen.

(*The snares begin a quiet, steady beat that builds in volume and intensity.*)

All those squats.

(**MIKE** *inches a little bit higher...*)

COACH. All those up-downs.

(*As* **YOUNG MIKE** *begins to inch in front of his teammates.*)

JERRY. You okay?

MIKE.	**COACH.**
I CAN DO THIS.	YOU CAN DO THIS.

(*One of the* **PLAYERS** *fails and is flung back to his starting point.*)

JERRY. Maybe that's enough.

MIKE. NO.

COACH. THERE IS A STRENGTH YOU HAVE NOT TAPPED.

> *(Another* **PLAYER** *fails and flies back.)*

MIKE. I'M NOT FINISHED.

COACH. FIGHT FOR IT.

MIKE. I'M NOT FINISHED.

COACH. EVERY INCH.

MIKE. I'M NOT FINISHED.

COACH. FIGHT FOR EVERY INCH OF YOUR LIFE.

> *(The snare drums suddenly stop...)*
>
> *(As the other two* **PLAYERS** *fly back to their starting positions.)*
>
> *(And now it's just* **YOUNG MIKE**, *inching toward the line.)*
>
> *(And* **MIKE**, *inching toward standing.)*
>
> *(***YOUNG MIKE** *reaches out toward that goal line, closer and closer...)*
>
> *(As* **MIKE***'s legs shake harder and harder.)*

JERRY. You're almost there, Mike, you're almost there.

> *(***YOUNG MIKE** *slides back a step, nearly falling all the way.)*

You're right there.

> *(***YOUNG MIKE** *catches himself.)*

You're doing great, just a few inches--

> *(***YOUNG MIKE** *screams a battle cry, then drives through the goal line, as the scoreboard lights up with another score.)*

MIKE. JESUS--STOP.

JERRY. Okay.

MIKE. PLEASE STOP.

JERRY. Okay.

JERRY & MARCUS. I got you.

JERRY. We're sitting down, okay?

MARCUS. Enjoy the ride.

> (**YOUNG MIKE** *lets himself fly back into* **MARCUS**' *arms...*)

> (*As* **JERRY** *guides* **MIKE** *back down.*)

JERRY. Okay, okay...

Hey.

Hey.

> (**JERRY** *begins to unstrap* **MIKE**...)

You did really well, Mike.

> (*As* **MARCUS** *unwraps the bungee from* **YOUNG MIKE**'s *waist.*)

YOUNG MIKE. You did, actually, you put up a good fight.

MIKE. *(Quietly.)* Shut up.

JERRY. You *did.*

YOUNG MIKE. *(Coming to* **MIKE**.*)* But the harder you try--

JERRY. This was just your first try--

YOUNG MIKE. The more you wish you were me.

MIKE. *(A bit louder.)* Will you shut the fuck up?

JERRY. Do *not* give up on me, Mike--

YOUNG MIKE. Oh I'm not giving up I'm just getting started--

JERRY. We will try this again--

YOUNG MIKE. I'm coming for you--

JERRY. And we'll keep trying--

YOUNG MIKE. And I'll keep coming--

JERRY. Until we get this--

YOUNG MIKE. Till you're *nothing*--

YOUNG MIKE.	**JERRY.**
Till you're *finished*--	You are not finished--

MIKE. GET THE FUCK OFF ME DO NOT FUCKING TOUCH ME!!

(Beat.)

*(***MIKE*** *uses his last remaining strength to wheel himself offstage...)*

(As the drum beats return, growing faster and louder...)

(Until lights burst up on ***DAMON****, dancing violently across the stage.)*

(Lights fade on all but him as the drums continue their assault, and ***DAMON*** *continues his assault on the stage.)*

(All the frustration, all the anger, all the resentment and guilt – everything that's been bottled up – it all comes out in this dance.)

(The dance builds to a frenzy...)

(As ***MIKE*** *enters, watching the final moments.)*

*(***DAMON*** *builds to a climax, but before he gets there...)*

(He slams his leg on the floor and takes a sharp intake of breath.)

(Softly.) Dad?

*(***DAMON*** *puts weight on the leg and goes down.)*

Dad--Jesus--Are you okay--

DAMON. I'm sorry.

MIKE. What?

DAMON. I'm sorry I thought you were sleeping--

MIKE. It's okay--

DAMON. Do you need anything?

MIKE. What?

DAMON. *(Trying to rise.)* Are you hungry?

MIKE. No--

DAMON. Are you thirsty--

MIKE. No, *Dad*--

DAMON. I'll get you something to...

> (**DAMON** *rises, but grimaces as soon as he puts weight on his ankle.*)

MIKE. I'll go get some ice.

DAMON. *I'll* get it.

MIKE. I got it--

DAMON. I can get it you shouldn't be--

MIKE. *(Sharply.)* Just let me do this, okay?!

> (**DAMON** *stops.*)
>
> *(Beat.)*

Just...

Just sit back down, okay?

> (**DAMON** *sits back down as* **MIKE** *goes to get some ice.*)
>
> *(Beat.)*
>
> (**DAMON** *puts his hand on his ankle, inhales sharply...*)
>
> *(As* **MIKE** *re-enters with a bag of ice.*)

You're too old to be moving like that.

DAMON. Yeah the body doesn't work the way it used...

> *(Stops himself. Beat.)*

I'm sorry.

MIKE. *(Coming to him.)* It's okay.

DAMON. That was an awful thing to say.

MIKE. Yeah, well, I'm deeply offended. Put your leg up.

DAMON. What?

MIKE. You need to elevate it.

DAMON. I can't put my leg on your--

MIKE. Just do it, old man.

> *(Beat.)*
>
> (**DAMON** *places his leg on Mike's leg, inhales sharply.*)

(Beat.)

*(**MIKE** helps his father adjust his leg until it's comfortable...)*

(Beat.)

(And then places the ice on his father's ankle.)

*(**DAMON** inhales when the ice hits his skin...)*

(Beat.)

(But then settles into it...)

(Let this establish.)

*(After a long while, **MIKE** begins to quietly cry.)*

(Beat.)

DAMON. Are you okay?

> *(Quick beat.)*

MIKE. *(Softly.)* I'm fine.

DAMON. *(Tries to move his leg.)* I'm sorry I--

MIKE. Just leave it, I just...

> *(Lights rise on another part of the stage...)*
>
> *(Where **YOUNG MIKE** ices down **MARCUS**.)*

YOUNG MIKE. Dislocated shoulder, broken pinky, six bruises and a stinger.

MARCUS. You braggin' or somethin'?

YOUNG MIKE. I'm just sayin'...

You should be icing *me* down.

> *(Beat.)*

MARCUS. Where's the sixth?

YOUNG MIKE. What?

MARCUS. I counted five bruises. Where's the sixth?

> *(Quick beat.)*

YOUNG MIKE. Play your cards right maybe you'll find out.

>> (**MARCUS** *looks at* **YOUNG MIKE**, *rolls his eyes at first...*)

>> (*But keeps looking at* **YOUNG MIKE**.)

What?

MIKE. Dad?

>> (*Beat.*)

I um...

>> (*Beat.*)

There was this...

>> (*Beat; in tears.*)

I had this teammate...

YOUNG MIKE. *What?*

MARCUS. (*Softer.*) Man what the fuck are we doin'?

>> (*Quick beat.*)

YOUNG MIKE. What are you talkin' a--

MARCUS. They're sayin' I'm goin' fifth round, at best, who the fuck's gonna draft me they find out--

YOUNG MIKE. Look don't worry about that--

>> (**MARCUS** *sucks in his breath.*)

And anyway that shit's changin'.

MARCUS. Changin' ain't *changed*. This is my *life*, you understand?

>> (*Beat.*)

YOUNG MIKE. Yeah, well...

>> (*Quick beat; with an edge.*)

I ain't goin' fifth round all right I'm goin' *first*.

MARCUS. You're goin' late second early third.

YOUNG MIKE. Oh fuck Mel Kiper--I'm goin' first round, *guaranteed contract*.

And you know what I'm gonna do with it?

>> (*Beat.*)

(No response.)

(Funny voice.)

YOUNG MIKE. Do you know what I am going to--

MARCUS. Jesus *what*?

(Quick beat.)

YOUNG MIKE. *(With a grin.)* I'm gonna get a little chateau. South of France.

*(**MARCUS** smirks; Quick beat.)*

Where no one gives a fuck.

*(**MARCUS** looks at **YOUNG MIKE**.)*

(Beat.)

You gonna be there?

(Beat.)

MARCUS. *(Trying to make a joke.)* You gonna have a pool?

*(**YOUNG MIKE** gives **MARCUS** a look, like, "Don't make a joke of this.")*

(Beat.)

(Then...)

(With naked vulnerability:)

YOUNG MIKE. Are you gonna be there?

*(**MARCUS** looks at **YOUNG MIKE**...)*

(And imagines the two of them, poolside.)

(He smiles wide – no strut, no front, just... happy.)

(He takes a breath that gets caught in his throat...)

(Then nods.)

MARCUS. Yeah.

*(**YOUNG MIKE** can't help but flash a big, toothy, stupid smile...)*

(Which he quickly covers.)

(He nods...)

(Then turns to **MIKE**.*)*

YOUNG MIKE. *Yeah.*

MIKE. That didn't...

(As **YOUNG MIKE** *rises.)*

We never got to--There was never any fucking chateau.

YOUNG MIKE. *(Moving to* **MIKE**.*)* Doesn't matter--I can see it.

I know how *my* story ends.

*(***YOUNG MIKE** *lands next to* **MIKE**.*)*

(He looks up at the scoreboard, as the clock ticks down to 0:00.)

Fourth quarter, friend.

(Quick beat.)

This is the part where I put my foot on your throat.

(Lights fade, as the clock resets to 15:00...)

FOURTH QUARTER

> *(... And then begins to tick down.)*
>
> *(Lights rise on **MIKE**, alone onstage.)*

JERRY. *(Offstage.)* I have a gift for you.

> *(**JERRY** enters, with a walker in his hands.)*
>
> *(He sets the walker in front of **MIKE** and awaits a reaction.)*
>
> *(There is none.)*

Oh, sorry.

> *(He sticks a bow on the walker and presents it again.)*
>
> *(Beat.)*

Nothing?

MIKE. I can't even stand.

JERRY. And that's why we're going to try again this afternoon.

MIKE. *(Sharply.)* Why do you...

> *(Stops himself.)*
>
> *(Quick beat.)*

JERRY. Why do I waste my time on you?

MIKE. You're kind of a pain in the ass, you know that?

JERRY. Yeah it's my approach.

MIKE. And isn't this exactly what you're *not* supposed to do?

JERRY. Excuse me?

MIKE. I've read the pamphlets--this is very un-PC of you-- Lifting up "the nobility of walking."

JERRY. You know what Mike?

MIKE. *What.*

JERRY. Fuck off.

> *(Quick beat.)*

I've got all kinds of clients I'm no better than a single one of them because I can walk--You've got an incomplete spinal injury, there's a chance you can stand. The question is whether you're willing to *work*.

> *(Beat.)*

What?

MIKE. You sounded like a football coach just now.

JERRY. Not all of us were star players at UT; doesn't mean we didn't play.

> *(Quick beat.)*

Just means we didn't play...particularly well.

> *(Quick beat.)*

MIKE. Is that why you work with football players?

JERRY. I work with football players because I love football.

MIKE. Everyone loves football--even people who don't know it yet.

JERRY. Yeah, but I see what it does.

> *(Beat.)*

MIKE. *(Softer.)* Your other clients...are they as bad as me?

> *(We hear the sound of athletic tape being pulled and ripped.)*

JERRY. I've got a guy...

> *(Lights rise on the **PLAYERS** taping themselves up for the game.)*

He's forty-four years old.

> *(One of the young **PLAYERS** rises...)*

Comes and sees me once a month and every time he sees me he has no idea who I am.

> *(The young **PLAYER** grabs his helmet, puts it on, takes the field.)*

I've got another guy, compressed sciatic nerve.

> *(Another young **PLAYER** rises...)*

Can't sleep more than two hours before the pain wakes him up.

> *(The young **PLAYER** puts on his helmet, takes the field.)*

I've got a C2 injury...

> *(Another young **PLAYER**...)*

A T4...

> *(Another young **PLAYER**.)*

A T7...

> *(Another.)*

An L2.

> *(Another.)*

(As the rest take the field.) And every Saturday I'm in those stands and every Sunday I'm in front of my TV so what does that say about me?

> *(Quick beat.)*

MIKE. Good taste.

> *(Quick beat.)*

JERRY. You didn't get hurt because you loved someone.

> *(**MIKE** looks at **JERRY**.)*

You got hurt 'cause you played a game that hurts people.

> *(Quick beat.)*

MIKE. And if I could take the field tomorrow I *would* so what does that say about me?

> *(Beat.)*

JERRY. That you miss it.

> *(Quick beat.)*

COACH. *(Entering.)* I tell you what I miss most, gentlemen.

>   *(Quick beat.)*

'Cause it sure isn't those up-downs.

>   *(Quick beat.)*

It's that first play of the game.

>   *(And the **PLAYERS** are back in the game's opening moment.)*

When the ball's in the air...

>   *(**MARCUS** and **YOUNG MIKE** gaze skyward.)*

And everything off the field dissolves away...
And for once you are fully present for a moment of your life.

>   *(**MARCUS** receives the ball.)*

The moment's here gentlemen it is right in front of you.

>   *(**YOUNG MIKE** looks at **MARCUS**, and then at the opposing **PLAYERS** in the distance.)*

Will you live inside it?

>   *(The **PLAYERS** move.)*

Will you be no place but here?

>   *(**YOUNG MIKE** levels the first; **MARCUS** jukes the second.)*

No time but now?

>   *(Another block; another spin move.)*

Will you live in this moment?

>   *(**YOUNG MIKE** drives at the defender and everything freezes at the point of contact.)*
>   *(Beat.)*
>   *(And the lights slowly transform...)*
>   *(Back to that flickering glow of the television screen.)*
>   *(**MIKE** has the remote in his hand...)*
>   *(And we're back in his house.)*

(Where he's once again watching the moment he got hurt.)

(Where, once again, he has paused at the point of contact.)

(Let us sit in this for several moments.)

(And then, finally:)

YOUNG MIKE. *(Whispers.)* This is the part where you hit rewind.

(Louder whisper.)

C'mon.

(Beat.)

C'mon man you know you never watch what happens next--Just hit rewind.

*(**MIKE** looks at his younger self, slightly shakes his head.)*

Don't.

*(**MIKE** lifts the remote.)*

You watch this what happens next?

(Quick beat.)

*(**YOUNG MIKE** moves out of his frozen position.)*

*(The rest of the **PLAYERS** remain frozen.)*

What happens?

*(**YOUNG MIKE** approaches **MIKE**.)*

What, you watch this--Have some big breakthrough?

*(**YOUNG MIKE** removes his helmet.)*

No.

*(**YOUNG MIKE** breathes in.)*

No, you watch this then Dad comes in and tucks you into bed.

*(He kneels down beside **MIKE**.)*

(Softer; warmer.) We stood up to him.

(A shared look.)

YOUNG MIKE. We did.

Not me--us--We did that, together.

MIKE. Yeah.

YOUNG MIKE. Hit rewind.

(Quick beat.)

We'll go anywhere you want to go.

(Snaps his fingers.)

Oklahoma State--Sophomore year.

*(**MIKE** grins in remembrance.)*

Yeah--Fuck Jerry, right?

(Mocking voice.)

"When you've stunned a city's worth into silence."

(Normal voice.)

It's not about shutting them up.

It's not about getting them to stand; it's about making them boo their own team.

(Quick beat.)

When you can ruin an entire year for a hundred thousand--"Well now that our season's shot we can enjoy all the sights of Stillwater."

(The two laugh.)

*(**YOUNG MIKE** looks at **MARCUS**.)*

Hit rewind.

(Quick beat.)

Take us back to the locker room.

(Quick beat.)

The showers.

That first time we saw him.

MIKE. Jesus.

YOUNG MIKE. Fucking disaster, right?

MIKE. Nearly got hard.

YOUNG MIKE. In front of the whole team.

MIKE & YOUNG MIKE. *(To talk down the erection.)* Donald Trump, Donald Trump, Donald Trump.

> *(They laugh quietly together.)*

YOUNG MIKE. Our body knew before we did.

> *(Beat.)*

Our body knew.

> *(Beat.)*

Feel.

> *(He takes* **MIKE***'s hand and puts it on his own erection.)*

Now feel.

> *(He takes* **MIKE***'s other hand and puts it on* **MIKE***'s diaper.)*

> *(Beat.)*

Let's just go back, okay?

> *(Beat.)*

> *(***MIKE*** nods slightly.)*

> *(Beat.)*

MIKE. Into position.

> *(Quick beat.)*

YOUNG MIKE. Yes sir.

> *(***YOUNG MIKE*** puts his helmet back on and gets into position...)*

> *(As* **MIKE** *raises the remote and is about to hit rewind...)*

> *(When he looks at* **MARCUS***.)*

> *(Beat.)*

> *(He wheels himself through the scene, so that he's next to the frozen image of* **MARCUS***...)*

*(Looking vulnerable, looking to **YOUNG MIKE** for help.)*

(Beat.)

*(**MIKE** places his hand on **MARCUS**' face...)*

(Beat.)

*(Then turns **MARCUS**' face downfield...)*

*(Away from the sacrifice **YOUNG MIKE** is about to make...)*

*(And toward the touchdown that **MARCUS** is about to score.)*

YOUNG MIKE. What are you doing?

MIKE. He never saw us.

YOUNG MIKE. Sure he did.

MIKE. He never saw what we did.

YOUNG MIKE. Of course he did.

MIKE. No.

(Quick beat.)

No, he never looked back.

*(**MIKE** raises the remote.)*

YOUNG MIKE. Don't--*Please.*

*(**MIKE** presses play.)*

(And we watch the hit, all the way through.)

*(We watch as **YOUNG MIKE**'s body goes limp.)*

*(We watch as the **PLAYER** he drills doubles over and falls on top of him.)*

*(We watch as **MARCUS** nails his tackler with a stiff-arm to break free.)*

(And if all the previous sequences have had a certain beauty despite their violence...)

(This moment has none.)

(This moment is awful.)

*(**YOUNG MIKE**'s defender tries to pop to his feet, but immediately goes back down and*

starts crawling on the floor like an infant, gasping for breath...)

(While MARCUS' tackler struggles not to vomit...)

(While the other PLAYERS struggle to stumble to their feet.)

(And then...)

(With an eruption...)

(YOUNG MIKE spits out a mouthful of blood.)

MARCUS!

(The PLAYERS turn to YOUNG MIKE.)

(They see him there, on his back.)

(And the PLAYERS stop moving.)

MARCUS!!

(But MARCUS is gone.)

MARCUS!!

COACH. *(Coming to him; taking his hand.)* I'm here, Mike, I'm right here.

YOUNG MIKE. *(Panicked.)* I can't feel...

COACH. You're okay it's okay--

YOUNG MIKE. I can't feel my fucking legs!

COACH. It's just a stinger, Mike, trainer's comin'--

YOUNG MIKE. *(Softer.)* Marcus I can't move my fucking--

COACH. Hey hey--You're gonna be fine, okay, you're *invincible.* Nothin' hurts you.

YOUNG MIKE. *(Softer.)* Just take my hand, okay, man?

(COACH looks down; he's already holding it.)

Will you just take my fuckin' hand?!

(MARCUS re-enters, at the corner of the stage, his helmet in his hand.)

Marcus?

(MARCUS moves toward YOUNG MIKE's side.)

(And the **PLAYERS**, *in unison, turn their bodies and lift their heads and look right at* **MARCUS***...)*

(Stopping **MARCUS** *in his tracks.)*

(Softer.)

YOUNG MIKE. I just want you to hold my hand, okay? That's it.

Just please, just...

Just hold my hand, okay man?

*(***COACH** *looks up at* **MARCUS***...)*

(And a look of recognition passes between them.)

Marcus?

(Quick beat.)

*(***MARCUS** *takes a knee with the rest of the* **PLAYERS** *and lowers his head.)*

(Quick beat.)

Marcus.

COACH. I'm here, Mike, I'm right by your side.

*(***COACH** *nods to his* **PLAYERS**, *and they rise and approach* **YOUNG MIKE**.*)*

*(***DAMON** *enters.)*

(He stands behind **MIKE**, *watching as* **COACH** *leans in and whispers something in* **YOUNG MIKE***'s ear...)*

(As the **PLAYERS** *form a back brace underneath* **YOUNG MIKE***'s body.)*

YOUNG MIKE. What's happening?

COACH. Just keep listening to me you listen to *me.*

*(***COACH** *continues to whisper in* **YOUNG MIKE***'s ear, and then...)*

*(***YOUNG MIKE** *is lifted into the air with a sharp intake of breath.)*

YOUNG MIKE. Just stay here, okay, man?

Okay?

Marcus, just please, just don't...

> *(And they walk off.)*
>
> *(Like a procession.)*
>
> *(Like a funeral.)*
>
> *(When they pass* **MARCUS**, *he doesn't follow.)*
>
> *(He remains statue-still...)*
>
> *(As the light on him transforms.)*
>
> *(Growing darker...)*
>
> *(Back to the light of the hotel room...)*
>
> *(Until* **MARCUS** *is just a silhouette.)*
>
> *(***DAMON*** approaches* **YOUNG MIKE**...*)*
>
> *(And then touches him on the shoulder.)*
>
> *(Beat.)*

DAMON. Has he ever...

> *(Beat.)*

Have you heard from him?

> *(***MARCUS*** rises and slowly approaches* **MIKE**.*)*
>
> *(He looks at* **MIKE** *– sees* **MIKE** *in his wheelchair.)*
>
> *(***MIKE*** looks right back at* **MARCUS**, *and then:)*

MIKE. No.

> *(***MARCUS*** puts on his helmet.)*
>
> *(He puts on his armor.)*
>
> *(And he walks offstage.)*
>
> *(Beat.)*
>
> *(And as* **MIKE** *begins to break down...)*
>
> *(***DAMON*** runs his hand down* **MIKE**'s *arm, and holds his forearm.)*
>
> *(Beat.)*
>
> *(***MIKE*** takes his father's hand and holds it to his heart.)*

(And very slowly, the two start to rediscover...)

(Or rather redefine...)

(A physical language.)

*(**DAMON** begins to move toward his son, and **MIKE** lets him in.)*

*(As **DAMON** places his chin on **MIKE**'s shoulder.)*

(And for a moment, the two share an embrace...)

*(Before **MIKE** starts to rock back and forth.)*

(And that's all that needs to be said.)

*(**DAMON** places his legs on either side of **MIKE**'s legs and squeezes them tight.)*

(The men move closer together, and once they're in position...)

Three...

(Beat.)

DAMON. Two...

(Beat.)

MIKE & DAMON. *One.*

(And as the final minute of the game begins to tick down, the two men rise...)

(Slowly and steadily, to standing.)

*(**MIKE** starts to hyperventilate, and **DAMON** starts to bring him down, but **MIKE** tells him – without words...)*

("I'm okay.")

("I'm okay.")

(The two men stay standing...)

(Bearing each other's weight.)

(Beat.)

*(And then **MIKE** sees his walker.)*

(Just a few feet away.)

(With the open field beyond it.)

*(And as his father holds the embrace, and **MIKE**'s breathing begins to slow, a wicked grin creeps across his face.)*

(Before the clock can get to 0:00...)

*(**MIKE** takes one big breath in...)*

(And breathes the game clock – and all the lights – out.)

End of Play

SOME (HOPEFULLY HELPFUL) SUGGESTIONS

After several workshops and productions of *Colossal*, I've learned a great deal about the unique opportunities and challenges that the play presents. While I don't wish to impinge on anyone's artistry or creativity, I'd love to help you troubleshoot some challenges that typically arise.

Gameclock

Don't tell the audience, but the quarters will *not* perfectly time out to fifteen minutes. (They're often closer to twelve or thirteen – though this will of course vary production to production.)

Please do *not* try to stretch the quarters out to fifteen minutes (*Colossal* gets its power from its compression and muscularity). Rather, you'll want to "cheat" the clock – jumping it forward thirty or forty-five seconds, two to three times a quarter, when the audience isn't looking. After several productions, we haven't had a single audience member catch us once. If you choose the right moments to cheat, they won't catch you either.

A final note on the gameclock/scoreboard: the clock is probably more important than the score. (In case it's not clear in the script, the final score – before Mike blows the scoreboard out – is 14-0. Young Mike [generally designated as "Visitor"] scores two touchdowns – once in the first quarter and once in the third.)

But the score is secondary to the clock, which is meant to work on several levels. If Mike doesn't complete a sit-to-stand before the clock runs out, he never will. But on a deeper level, if he doesn't find a way to move forward before the clock expires, he'll become one of those ghosts who trolls the sidelines on game day. A fifty-year-old man perpetually reliving his twenty-year-old glory.

I'd encourage you to prioritize the clock over the score in the design.

Movement

For the inaugural production at Olney Theatre Center, I was so lucky to work with an entire *team* of experts to realize the physical vocabulary of the play. Choreographer Christopher D'Amboise handled the halftime show, Damon's solo, and all of Damon's movement. Fight and Movement Choreographer Ben Cunis developed much of the football/athletic movement, and a high school football coach served as our expert eye. On top of that, Director Will Davis is an absolute master of physical theatre, with an aesthetic that is kinetic, visceral, and precise.

It often takes a village to realize the movement of *Colossal*. But when done well, fully-fleshed characters will emerge through their physical vocabularies. When done well, professional football players, dancers, and physical therapists will come to the play and say, "You nailed it." *Colossal* should never feel like actors pretending to be athletes or dancers. They should embody the ferocity, violence, and precision of football and dance.

Dance

The two notes I seem to always give for the halftime show are: The performance should be shorter, and there should be more of an emphasis on the duet between Damon and Young Mike.

Five minutes seems to be an ideal length for the halftime show. After six or seven, the play generally starts to deflate – and *Colossal* needs to feel pressurized to the point of combustible.

Narratively speaking, the halftime show is all about the pas de deux between Damon and Young Mike. It's helpful to see the aesthetic of the Damon Shaw Dance Company (and I'd encourage an aesthetic that is as visceral and physical as football) – but it's the duet that establishes the relationship between father and son. It's the duet that allows us to see Mike through Damon's eyes. It's the duet that sets up the end of the play.

Ultimately, *Colossal* isn't just about Mike's struggle to move forward in the wake of trauma. As Mike Thornton (who originated the role of Mike) put it, "Everyone in this play has been paralyzed by the injury." If the end of the play is ultimately a father and son finding a new normal – then the halftime show is the old normal that must be grieved; the shared and intimate physical language that must now be redefined.

Football

One of the best pieces of advice I ever received from a former NFL player was, "You need to get that *pop*." By which he meant we needed to capture the sound that a football player experiences when he gets hit. The pads will be your friends here. You must enlist an expert to ensure that all hits are done safely, but people will get hit in this play. Helmets, pads, and mouthguards are essential.

Having said that, please do not feel compelled to always (or even often) choose the literal/realistic representation of football. A few quick examples:

The kickoff (in Quarters One and Four) looks potentially silly when the ball actually flies through the air. One option is to have the players articulate the flight path of the ball with their bodies – I've seen this done to extraordinary effect.

Another example: in one of Will Davis' productions, he realized the weight room sequence without actually using weights. Or rather – Young Mike/Marcus literally squatted with weights, but all of the other players performed rigorous exercises using the weight of each other's bodies. This looked gorgeous – was intensely physical and exhausting – and allowed the play to *move* at a pressurized pace (without slowing down to drag weights on and off stage, etc.).

Also, for clarification – in Quarter Two, the boys put Young Mike through "the gauntlet" to prove himself. There's an actual football drill called a gauntlet, and it's slightly different than what's intended here.

Young Mike simply needs to make it from one end of the field to the other without getting tackled. Creating a fairly narrow alley will help you here.

One last note on football: In your costume design, I'd encourage you to consider options where the players wear pads, but do *not* wear jerseys over them. So much of this play is about armor, and the pads serve as a beautiful evocation of this armor. Jerseys tend to look baggy and soft, and there is *no* room for sogginess in *Colossal*.

Speaking of...

Beats, Quick Beats, and Double-Dashes

Colossal is very carefully scored. The collision of interruptions and silence gives the play its musculature, and I consider those pesky beats and double-dashes to be as sacrosanct as dialogue. If you don't honor them, you're not doing the play. Period.

That said, the beats arent there simply to give the play shape through silence. It's about what's *happening* in that silence – what the characters are so often trying and failing to say. Coach's first scene with Mike is quite simply a father trying to tell his son he loves him, that he's so sorry this has happened, and that he wishes he could do so much more than simply give Mike a token position as a safety consultant.

It's a lot to communicate (or fail to communicate) in silence – but it's that struggle that will *activate* those beats, that will help pressurize the play, and that will deepen these characters.

The Role of Mike

As stated on the first page, the character of Mike must be played by an artist with a disability. That's non-negotiable. However, I'm less insistent that the disability must be a spinal injury, so if you have a specific question, please reach out to the publisher.

As with football, I'd encourage you to invite an expert on spinal injury rehab into the room (most likely a physical therapist).

The role of Mike was originally written for a specific actor and built around his body. So a couple of the exercises that are mentioned – the TKEs, for example – were tailored to that actor. Feel free to adapt the physical therapy sessions during Quarters One and Two as you see fit, and to better suit the actor playing Mike.

What *is* essential is that the exercises you choose are difficult/physically rigorous. Everyone in this play gets exhausted – including Mike. And one of the biggest traps of *Colossal* is to play Mike as detached and melancholic. Rather, he's a young man bottling extraordinary rage and pain – he's just lost so many of his previous outlets to express that passion and pain.

One important point: While the actor playing Mike may have a complete spinal injury, the character of Mike has an incomplete injury. So it is important that Mike and Jerry attempt a sit-to-stand in Quarter Three, even if it's an exercise that the actor is technically unable to perform. There are ways to "fake" this safely, and to great effect.

It's less vital that Mike and Damon perform a successful sit-to-stand at the end of the play – particularly if a sit-to-stand is not part of the actor's physical vocabulary.

The final moment of *Colossal* is not a triumph because Mike stands. It's a triumph because Mike and Damon learn to share each other's weight. It's about two men being present and vulnerable with each other, finding and redefining a new physical language, and bravely moving into the present tense of their lives.

I've seen productions that ended with a successful sit-to-stand; I've seen ones that ended with a trust fall, an embrace, a redefined pas de deux. All of these can work beautifully.

Final Thoughts
I set *Colossal* at the University of Texas in part because it's where I went to grad school (with our theatre department literally in the shadow of the football stadium) – and in part because I consider Texas the epicenter of American football: One of the few places where it's in the bloodstream at every level, from Pop Warner to professional.

That said, I'd discourage you from using Texas accents or going too wild with the UT paraphernalia/references. This play is at its best when it feels universal.

Also – there are a couple moments (in the weight room and in the gauntlet) where the players are encouraged to ad-lib. Have fun with this, but *please* – don't add any additional derogatory words (particularly racist or homophobic slurs). It may feel true to the football culture, but in the end – my name's attached to this play and there are certain words that I *never* use in any of my plays.

Last thought: At roughly seventy minutes (or less), *Colossal* is merciless. It should feel merciless for both the audience and the artists involved.

I've often said that if you suck in all your breath and tighten every muscle in your body – *that's* how the play should feel.

This is the most exhausting piece of theatre I've ever been a part of. But largely for that reason, it's probably the most rewarding. I thank you for taking this piece on – and if you ever have a question – don't hesitate to drop me a line.

– Andrew